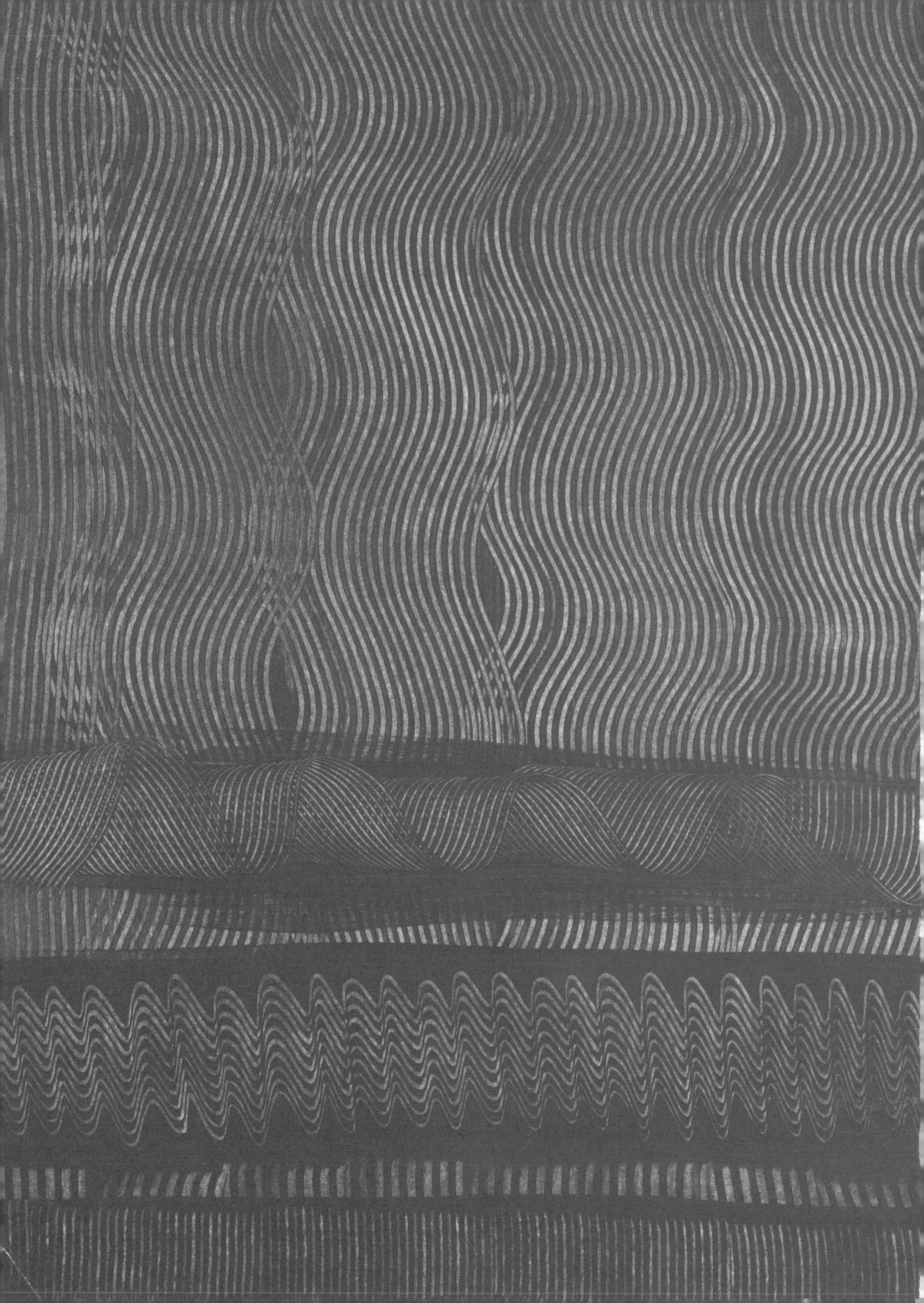

THE Impudent ROOSTER

Adapted by SABINA I. RĂSCOL
FROM A ROMANIAN STORY BY ION CREANGĂ

Illustrated by HOLLY BERRY

DUTTON CHILDREN'S BOOKS • NEW YORK

The Impudent Rooster is based on a story by Ion Creangă titled "*Punguța cu doi bani*" ["The Pouch with Two Coins"], first published in the January 1876 issue of the Romanian literary journal *Convorbiri literare* [*Literary Conversations*]. Romania's most esteemed and beloved storyteller, as well as a teacher and for a time a deacon in the Romanian Orthodox Church, Creangă wrote many stories and some autobiographical works, chief of which is his *Amintiri din copilărie* [*Memories from Childhood*]. He was friends with Mihai Eminescu, Romania's foremost poet; it was Eminescu who encouraged him to write. Creangă's works are appreciated for their humor and realism, and he is credited with raising Romanian folklore to the level of literature. "His masterpieces are the epic of the Romanian people," one critic said. "Creangă is our Homer." He was born March 1, 1837 (some say June 10, 1839), and died on December 31, 1889. While readers of Creangă's original tale will find here the story they love, they will encounter a kinder interpretation of the old man and old woman, a few new plot twists, and wordplay made possible by the English language. I hope this version will be as enjoyable to read as it was to write. —S.I.R.

Library of Congress Cataloging-in-Publication Data
Răscol, Sabina.
The impudent rooster: a Romanian folktale/retold by Sabina Răscol;
illustrated by Holly Berry. — 1st ed.
p. cm.
Summary: Using his amazing swallowing ability, a rooster foils the evil plans of a greedy nobleman and brings back riches to his poor master.
ISBN 0-525-47179-0
[1. Roosters — Folklore. 2. Folklore — Romania.]
I. Berry, Holly, ill. II. Title.
PZ8.1.R2246Im 2004
398.2'09498'04528625 — dc21 [E] 2003053141

Published in the United States by Dutton Children's Books,
a division of Penguin Young Readers Group
345 Hudson Street, New York, New York 10014
www.penguin.com
Designed by Sara Reynolds
First Edition
Manufactured in China
1 3 5 7 9 10 8 6 4 2

The illustrations for this book are done in watercolors
and colored pencils on rag paper.

To my family–
every last one of them. *Familiei mele.*
S.I.R.

With love to Phil–
a wonderful storyteller, teacher, and friend
H.B.

THERE ONCE LIVED

an old woman  and an old man. 

The old woman lived in a sturdy little house and kept a hen. The old man lived nearby in a tumbledown shack and kept a rooster.

The old man had worked hard his entire life, but as he grew old, he became ill and lost all he had. Now he was very poor. Sometimes he went for days on end eating nothing but cornmeal mush. The rooster was his only friend.

The old woman had eggs to eat and to sell, often passing her neighbor's ramshackle house with a full basket on the way to market. But though she saw the old man growing thinner and paler, she never offered him so much as one egg.

One day when the old man didn't have even cornmeal in the house, he stopped by the old woman's gate. "Neighbor," said he, "could you spare an egg for me? It would strengthen me, and then I could work. You'd be doing a good deed!"

But the old woman called him a beggar and shrilly advised, "Why don't you beat your rooster? I beat my hen, and see, I have plenty to eat!"

The old man loved his rooster. Every morning he smoothed the rooster's feathers, and every evening he kissed the rooster's comb. And now to hurt him? The old man could not think of it. But humiliated and weak from hunger, he snapped at the rooster, "I wish you were a hen and could lay eggs! I'm tired of being hungry!"

The rooster had always been the old man's pride and joy. At these words, the rooster lurched through the gate and took to the road, not knowing or caring where he went. After a while, his steps slowed, and he pecked in the soft earth near the road for something to eat. He pecked here, he pecked there, and then he saw something bright peeking through the fallen leaves. He pecked and he pulled, and up came a bright little purse with a few pennies in it. The rooster crowed, took the purse in his beak, and joyfully turned homeward. Now his master could buy some food!

Just then a coach swept by. Inside was a nobleman—a very rich, greedy nobleman who had amassed his wealth by wronging others. When he saw the purse in the rooster's beak, he called out, "Coachman! Stop! Catch that rooster and bring me the purse he's carrying!" And that's what the coachman did. Oh, how the rooster fought! But still he lost the bright little purse.

Then, "Drive on!" the nobleman commanded, and he leaned back against the cushions of the coach, happy to have added even those few pennies to his enormous wealth.

The rooster was dismayed to lose his newfound money. Oh, what could he do? He shook himself, beat his wings, and ran after the coach, crowing:

Cucurigu, my great lord!
Give back the pennies you stole!

The nobleman, surprised to see the rooster keeping up with the coach, didn't like what he heard. Oh, what impudence, that a rooster should call him a thief! When he spied a well on the side of the road, he had an idea. "Coachman! Stop!" he called out. "Catch that impudent rooster and throw him in the well!"

And that's what the coachman did. Oh, how the rooster fought! But down the well he went. He felt air rushing past him, saw the well's cool darkness, and then—*splash*, he plunged into the water. Floundering, about to drown, WHAT COULD THE ROOSTER DO? He drank sips, he drank slurps, he drank gulps. He drank and he drank until the well was dry. Then he beat his wings, flew out of the well, and ran until he caught up with the coach. As he ran, he crowed:

Cucurigu, my great lord!
Give back the pennies you stole!

The greedy nobleman hadn't expected to hear the rooster again. Oh, what impudence, that a rooster should call him a thief! And then he had another idea. As soon as he arrived home, he called out, "Cook! Fire the oven hot, then fire it hotter. Catch that impudent rooster and throw him in!"

And that's what the cook did. Oh, how the rooster fought! But into the oven he went. Flames singed the rooster's feathers. Glowing wood burned his feet. Hot air choked him. WHAT COULD THE ROOSTER DO?

He spouted out gulps, he spurted out slurps, he spit out sips, until he poured out all the water he'd drunk in the well.

The fire sizzled and hissed and fizzled out. Water flowed through the nobleman's house. Then the rooster beat his wings, pushed aside the oven grating, and flew out. He knocked with his beak on the nobleman's door and crowed:

Cucurigu, my great lord!
Give back the pennies you stole!

The greedy nobleman was amazed to see the rooster again. Oh, what impudence, that a rooster should call him a thief! So he thought and thought and had another idea. He called out, "Steward! Catch that impudent rooster and lock him in the money room. Let him stay there until he starves to death!"

And that's what the steward did. Oh, how the rooster fought! But he ended up alone amidst stacks of coins and sacks of treasure. The walls closed in. Piles of money shifted and fell, nearly burying him. WHAT COULD THE ROOSTER DO? He began to gobble coins. He gobbled small coins, big coins, silver and gold. He gobbled and gobbled until the room was empty.

Then the rooster beat his wings, knocked down the barred door, and flew out of the room. He clinked with his beak on the nobleman's window and crowed:

Cucurigu, my great lord!
Give back the pennies you stole!

The greedy nobleman could not believe that the rooster was back. Oh, what impudence, that a rooster should call him a thief! Again he thought and thought how to end the rooster's pestering. Finally an idea came to him. He called out, "Herdsman! Catch that impudent rooster and throw him in the middle of my herd so that the cattle will gore him or trample him!"

And that's what the herdsman did. Oh, how the rooster fought!

But he ended up in the middle of the herd, among great beasts with sharp horns and rushing hooves. WHAT COULD THE ROOSTER DO? He began to swallow. He swallowed bulls, he swallowed oxen, he swallowed cows and calves, until he had swallowed the entire herd. Then he shook himself, beat his wings, and strode out of the pasture.

The rooster was now as big as a hill, and when he stood outside the nobleman's house, he blocked the light of the sun. He crowed:

Cucurigu, my great lord!
Give back the pennies you stole!

The greedy nobleman, aghast to see the rooster again, was at his wit's end. Oh, what nerve! What utter impudence! Once more, he pondered how to be rid of the rooster. He had only one idea, and he didn't like it.

He shouted and stomped and shook his fist. No, not one bit did he like his idea! But what could he do? He was out of ideas. So the greedy nobleman took the bright little purse with its few pennies and threw it to the rooster.

The rooster, crowing delightedly, picked up the purse in his beak and marched off the nobleman's estate. As he stepped over the great iron gates, all the nobleman's poultry—hens and roosters, ducks and drakes, guinea hens and cocks, geese and ganders, turkey hens and cocks—awed by the rooster's size and courage and amazing deeds, followed him.

The greedy nobleman shook his fist when he saw that his birds were leaving. He shook his fist and shouted when he thought of his herd. He shouted and stamped both feet when he thought of his silver and gold. He called his servants and commanded them to stop the rooster. But the servants knew they couldn't—and wouldn't. The nobleman was now too poor to pay them.

The steward said, "You have no more silver or gold."

The herdsman said, "Your entire herd is gone."

The cook said, "Your poultry have all followed the rooster."

So the servants left the greedy nobleman, and from that time on, he had to work for a living and take care of himself, as other people did.

As for the rooster, he walked proudly toward the old man's house. The birds behind him overflowed the road, and such crowing and cackling and clucking and quacking and hissing and gobbling and honking and squawking rose in the air that people in their yards and houses stopped their work to look at the extraordinary procession.

When the rooster arrived at the old man's house, he began to crow:

Cucurigu! Cucurigu! Cucurigu!

The old man had been very sad since his rooster had left. Hearing his crow, the old man came out crying with joy. How he had missed his friend! He embraced the rooster, although he hardly recognized him, now grown so big and surrounded by this multitude of birds.

The old man asked the rooster's forgiveness for his ill-tempered words, and the rooster rubbed his head against the old man's hand. He had long since forgiven his master.

"Now, master, we have some work to do," the rooster said. "Open the gate to the pasture and lay out a large cloth in the house." And so the old man did. Then the rooster beat his wings, and the pasture filled with cattle—oxen, bulls, cows, and lowing calves. He beat his wings again, and a pile of coins

appeared—big, small, silver, gold—nearly blinding the old man. As the yard filled with fowls, the pasture with cattle, and the old run-down house with coins, the old man was overcome. He walked around in a daze, crying, hugging the rooster, and thanking him.

During this time, the old woman had been looking across the road and gnashing her teeth with envy. She put on the kerchief that she wore on Sundays and holidays and went to visit the old man. "Good day, neighbor," she greeted him in honeyed tones. "How wonderful to see you prospering! Tell me, how did all this wealth find you? Maybe some will find me, too!"

The old man answered, "You don't remember? You told me to mistreat my rooster. Well, I did. But he forgave me and brought all these riches back."

The old woman returned to her house and shouted to her hen, "Hey, hen! Leave, and don't return until you too can bring me something fine!" The hen, who had never been treated kindly by the old woman, gladly flew out of the yard and into the fields. From there, she joined the old man's fowls and lived on happily in their midst.

The old man built a large house and bought some fine clothes. He used his wealth to provide for poor people for miles around. He even helped the old woman when she needed it.

The rooster accompanied the old man everywhere. He wore a gold collar and yellow boots with spurs and looked as splendid as a king's son. Until the end of his days, he amazed everybody with his courage. But after all, THERE WAS NOTHING ELSE THAT THE ROOSTER COULD DO.